Once Removed

by

Eduardo Machado

SAMUEL
FRENCH

FOUNDED 1830

NEW YORK HOLLYWOOD LONDON TORONTO

SAMUELFRENCH.COM

ISBN 978-0-573-66046-7   Printed in U.S.A.   #17728

IMPORTANT BILLING AND CREDIT REQUIREMENTS

All producers of *ONCE REMOVED* *must* give credit to the Author of the Play in all programs distributed in connection with performances of the Play, and in all instances in which the title of the Play appears for the purposes of advertising, publicizing or otherwise exploiting the Play and/or a production. The name of the Author *must* appear on a separate line on which no other name appears, immediately following the title and *must* appear in size of type not less than fifty percent of the size of the title type.

ONCE REMOVED was produced at the Coconut Grove Playhouse in Miami, Florida on April 5th, 2003. The production was directed by Michael John, with set design by Steve Lambert, lighting design by Eric Nelson, costume design by Ellis Tillman, and sound design by Steve Shapiro. The cast was as follows:

OLGA	Lucie Arnaz
FERNANDO	Gary Perez
BARBARA	Flora Diaz
ROLANDO	Gilbert Cruz
ROSITA	Lourdes Martin

For my Mother and Father,
Gilda and Othon

ACT ONE

Hialeah, 1960. The living room of a very small bunga-
low. The only furniture on stage is a couch. The couch is
old and too big for the room. On the floor there is a black
phone, it is ringing. **OLGA,** *a very well-dressed woman,*
is standing next to the phone. Not knowing what to do,
she reaches to pick it up, but can't. She does the sign of
the cross. The phone rings again.

BARBARA. Pick it up! Mama!

OLGA. I can't.

BARBARA. Why?

OLGA. It might be an American!

    (**BARBARA** *rushes over to the phone and picks it up.*)

BARBARA. Hello? They hung up.

OLGA. See, it wasn't important.

BARBARA. It could have been grandma.

OLGA. No believe me, it was not La Habana.

BARBARA. How do you know?

OLGA. Cuba has a different ring.

BARBARA. Why did we have to come here?

OLGA. You know why. Fidel Castro! May he get a brain
tumor in the middle of a speech.

BARBARA. Right. Fidel Castro.

OLGA. Barbara, I'll show you a little bit of home.

BARBARA. Our treasure? Yes, Mama.

OLGA. Lock the doors.

BARBARA. They're locked. No one knows we have a
treasure.

OLGA. They suspect we do. They know who we are.

BARBARA. No one around here knows us. Believe me,

they're either Cubans from Matanzas –

OLGA. They know who my father is in Matanzas.

BARBARA. Or Yankees.

OLGA. I have a past. You have a past.

(The telephone rings. **OLGA** *goes to pick it up.)*

BARBARA. Good, Mama.

*(***OLGA** *picks up the telephone. Then hangs it up. Then puts it off the hook.)*

OLGA. No more interruptions.

BARBARA. Show them to me. Make me happy.

*(***OLGA** *opens the small suitcase, it is filled with a vast array of jewelry. She and* **BARBARA** *fondle various items.)*

BARBARA. Oh.

OLGA. Ay!

BARBARA. Oh.

OLGA. Sweet.

BARBARA. Bright.

OLGA. Yes.

BARBARA. They make me so happy.

OLGA. Our past.

BARBARA. They're so beautiful.

OLGA. Stones. Gold. Solid.

BARBARA. Real.

OLGA. Relics.

BARBARA. Ours!

OLGA. It was worth it. Smuggling them.

BARBARA. Why didn't we get out some photos with the jewels?

OLGA. Believe me dear, even the smallest photo wouldn't have fit into some of the places where I hid these gems. These are our only mementos. We must cherish them and...

BARBARA. Must be sixty thousand dollars worth.

OLGA. More...

BARBARA. Why don't we sell them and move to the Fontainebleau Hotel?

OLGA. Because our heritage is not for sale! I only care about their emotional value. This wedding ring proves that your father loves me. This emerald cross is a testament to my grandmother's belief in The Holy Catholic Church!

BARBARA. And in emeralds.

OLGA. If I die, promise that you will never sell them.

BARBARA. I promise.

OLGA. Your father is lifting bricks and God knows what else for a living. But we promised each other that this, our heritage, will stay with us. Castro may have taken away our business, our church, our nuns and our priest, but the jewelry we kept.

BARBARA. And on my fifteenth birthday. When I come out?

OLGA. At the yacht club. We are throwing your party at the La Habana yacht club.

BARBARA. We will be back by then?

OLGA. Of course. This will all be over in the next couple of months.

BARBARA. When I come out. I'll get to wear French couture, yes?

OLGA. Yes, and we will introduce you to whatever of our society is left.

(**OLGA** *kisses one of the bracelets.*)

OLGA. My father bought this for me. I miss him.

BARBARA. I miss grandma.

(**BARBARA** *points at a set of pearl earrings.*)

BARBARA. She gave me these, right?

OLGA. As soon as you were born she ran to get your ears pierced. Then she bought a set of little pearls and another set identical but bigger for when you come out.

BARBARA. Let me wear the big ones now.

OLGA. When you're fifteen.

BARBARA. It's only eight months away.

OLGA. My engagement ring. It was a decade of jewelry. Then... Then... then...

BARBARA. Revolution? How are we having our Spam today?

OLGA. Fried. Fried Spam.

BARBARA. You'd think the Catholic Relief would give you something besides Spam...

OLGA. Let's not talk about Spam.

BARBARA. ...Velveeta Cheese and lima beans.

OLGA. Why do you always have to bring us down to reality?

BARBARA. Sorry.

OLGA. I'm so depressed.

BARBARA. Don't worry. We'll go back. Real soon.

OLGA. We'll beat that son of a bitch!

BARBARA. Yes we will.

OLGA. Look at this, look at the diamond in this pin.

(**OLGA** *starts to cry.*)

OLGA. You see clear inside, no little piece of carbon. I can't control myself today. Sorry. I have to put them away. They bring back too many memories. So much pain. *(She touches her stomach.)* Did we deserve it? I ask you, Barbara, did we?

BARBARA. I wonder what stranger is playing with my doll house now?

OLGA. I'm sure your Aunt Rosita put it in hiding.

(A knock on the front door, **OLGA** *freezes.)*

OLGA. Yankees!

*(**OLGA** starts to put the jewels back into the briefcase. The knocking starts again.)*

OLGA. Help me! Help me!

ROLANDO. Don't hide the jewels!

OLGA. They know who we are! They know what we are doing! See, the FBI! Run! Hide it! Don't drop any!

ROLANDO. It's your cousin Rolando. Let me in, for Christ's sake.

BARBARA. It's a relative, thank God. It's a relative.

(BARBARA goes to door.)

OLGA. No. Put them away first. I don't want him to know how many of them we got out.

BARBARA. You're the one that knows the hiding place.

OLGA. Right. I'll put them away. You open the door. We'll be right there, cousin.

ROLANDO. Fine. Make me wait!

(OLGA exits to the bedroom. BARBARA opens the door. ROLANDO enters, he is wearing sporty clothes and carrying a grocery bag.)

ROLANDO. Been washing dishes all day long, then I have to wait to get into my cousin's house.

BARBARA. Sorry.

ROLANDO. I mean my life's ambition was not to be a dishwasher.

(He hands BARBARA the grocery bag.)

ROLANDO. Here, a present for my goddaughter.

BARBARA. It's not Easter.

(BARBARA looks inside the bag.)

BARBARA. Pantry Pride. From Pantry Pride? You bought me chocolates?

(OLGA enters.)

OLGA. Rolando, water?

ROLANDO. Of course, Olga. From the refrigerator.

OLGA. Chilled. I keep it in a bottle and everything.

(BARBARA takes out a costume from a five-and-dime store.)

BARBARA. You want me to be a clown?

OLGA. Are they having a carnival?

ROLANDO. Not really.

OLGA. Mardi Gras?

ROLANDO. No, it's for this thing the Americans do today.

OLGA. Thank him anyway, Barbara.

BARBARA. Thank you. What do I do with it?

ROLANDO. Halloween. Haven't you heard about it?

BARBARA. It has something to do with witches.

OLGA. I don't want her to have anything to do with witches!

ROLANDO. No, you go out dressed up in a costume. You say some kind of saying. "Treat the tricks." That's it. My children are going. You should go.

OLGA. She doesn't want to.

ROLANDO. It's a tradition here.

OLGA. She doesn't want to "Treat the tricks."

ROLANDO. It's good enough for my children.

OLGA. You children have been here for a year.

BARBARA. They're getting American...

OLGA. She's only been here for three months.

BARBARA. I'm still Cuban.

OLGA. Good.

ROLANDO. What's good enough for my children is good enough for your daughter.

BARBARA. What?

OLGA. Barbara!

ROLANDO. It's a tradition. Have fun. My kids say you get candy.

OLGA. Rolando! You know what they say about Gringos and candy. Have your wife and you lost all sense of reality?

ROLANDO. This is my idea. It has nothing to do with my wife!

(**FERNANDO** *is heard screaming.*)

FERNANDO. Ay! Ay! Olga!

OLGA. Fernando!

(**BARBARA** *goes outside.*)

BARBARA. Papi? What's wrong? Papi.

(**BARBARA** *reenters with* **FERNANDO**, *he is limping.*)

FERNANDO. I broke my back doing menial work

OLGA. Leave the room, Barbara. I don't want you to see the sacrifices your father is making for you.

ROLANDO. Take your costume, try it on.

(**BARBARA** *exits with the bag.*)

FERNANDO. Look at my hands. Look at my hands.

OLGA. And those hands used to be manicured.

FERNANDO. My God, my back is split in half!

ROLANDO. Can you move your toes?

FERNANDO. I can't move anything.

(**FERNANDO** *cries.*)

ROLANDO. Fernando, shit. Don't cry in front of your wife. If you cry in front of your wife, it's all over.

FERNANDO. What?

ROLANDO. Manhood.

OLGA. His hands were so smooth. You could tell he was special. Not one day of hard labor on them. And now... Now...Now they're common.

FERNANDO. The telephone! Jesus Christ. Will you hang up the dammed telephone.

OLGA. It was you who was calling?

FERNANDO. I needed help walking. It hurts, sweetie. It hurts.

OLGA. I'm so sorry.

FERNANDO. This exile is not what I expected.

OLGA. Me either.

ROLANDO. Actually this is pretty much what I thought it would be like.

OLGA. And you came anyway?

ROLANDO. Could not stay in a country run by a communist.

FERNANDO. Lousy bastard. I knew it the first day I met Fidel. I was having a cocktail at the yacht club. I was, of course, wearing white. Then, I am introduced to this punk wearing a green sports coat.

ROLANDO. Fidel?

FERNANDO. Fidel Castro.

OLGA. How dare he.

FERNANDO. Imagine a green sports coat at the yacht club.

OLGA. Social climber, that's all he was.

ROLANDO. You should have shot him when you had the chance.

FERNANDO. He wanted to be a baseball player back then,

ROLANDO. If only the Major Leagues would have taken him. I wouldn't be washing dishes at the Hilton.

OLGA. No, you'd be selling sandwiches at your roadside stand.

ROLANDO. But Fidel Castro did not have a good enough batting average. A country's destiny destroyed by a lousy batting average. Is that fair?

OLGA. In Cuba you would have been washing dishes at your stand. What's the difference, for someone like you?

ROLANDO. I would own the dishes I was washing.

FERNANDO. We got a bad break, that's for sure, Rolando.

ROLANDO. No. I am not going to let exile smother my economic potential.

FERNANDO. Good for you.

ROLANDO. I am going to save enough money for a deposit on a house. Fix the house up myself. A little bit of paint. Give it a little bit of Cuban class. Turn it around in a few years, sell it for a profit. Buy two other houses with the profits and so on and so on...

OLGA. You think you could make a house like this one have class?

ROLANDO. With the r_ght paint. The right bathroom fixtures, sure. I'll make a bundle out of this exile.

OLGA. I used to read romantic novelettes and in those books, exile was an aristocratic city where kings and countesses went. 'Till the hard times were over. An exotic place where you were sent to forget a lover or a fiancé who had played with your emotions. But never some dirty town next to Miami. Only known in the world for its dog races. Not this place. Not Hialeah!

FERNANDO. We are leaving Hialeah.

OLGA. What? We're going back to Cuba! I'll pack my bag.

ROLANDO. Wait a minute, that would make you traitors –

OLGA. No, we'll go back and work for the underground, and wait for that army that you Batistianos are forming in –

ROLANDO. Don't talk too loudly about the army. It's supposed to be a secret!

OLGA. Come back with us.

ROLANDO. I'm only going back there with a gun and a hand grenade

FERNANDO. We are not going back to Cuba!

OLGA. We're not?

FERNANDO. Is she slowly losing all sense of reality?

ROLANDO. Imagine how hard it must be for the women. Especially someone like Olga who was used to the finer things in life: a chauffeur, a maid.

OLGA. I don't miss the maids! Damn it! But, I did not come here to end up as somebody else's maid! I am not of that class!

ROLANDO. This is the USA, cousin. They don't have classes.

FERNANDO. Everybody is equal. That's right. You make your own choices. That's democracy.

ROLANDO. Yeah!

OLGA. My own choices?

FERNANDO. That's right.

OLGA. So where are you going to force me to live?

FERNANDO. Dallas, Texas.

OLGA. I am not going to Dallas, Texas.

FERNANDO. You are going with me!

OLGA. My sister needs me to be here waiting for her.

FERNANDO. It's going to be months before your sister gets an exit visa.

OLGA. That's not true. They already did Rosita's inventory. Once the block committee sees my sister's clothes, they'll want her out of there fast. It's gonna kill her.

FERNANDO. What?

OLGA. Giving up her wardrobe. My sister lives for those clothes.

FERNANDO. I can't sit around waiting for her. I need a job.

OLGA. You have a job.

FERNANDO. Had a job.

ROLANDO. You lost it?

FERNANDO. I quit.

ROLANDO. How could you?

FERNANDO. Do you think I was raised to lift ten bricks at a time? All day long.

ROLANDO. No, but necessity makes strange bedfellows.

FERNANDO. I have a mind. A mind that should be used to make money.

OLGA. I am only packing my bags to go home to Cuba. Do you understand me, Fernando? Either Cuba or nowhere.

FERNANDO. We are going to Dallas, Texas, cause I say so, God dammit!

ROLANDO. How did you get the tickets?

FERNANDO. Well...

ROLANDO. Catholic Relief?

FERNANDO. No.

OLGA. No?

FERNANDO. Presbyterians.

OLGA. What Presbyterians?

FERNANDO. Presbyterians from Texas.

OLGA. Where did you meet them?

FERNANDO. I went to their relief.

ROLANDO. A Presbyterian Relief?

FERNANDO. It's right next door to the Catholic one. It's the office next door. I heard they had more money.

OLGA. If I'm getting relief, I am getting it from my own religion.

FERNANDO. Your religion had given all its relief away. The Presbyterians are organizing a new program. They'll relocate us –

ROLANDO. They want to get us out of Miami. I knew it! We are going to be put into camps next.

OLGA. Nobodies, that's what we are. Why didn't we stay? Live in our country, with the communists?

FERNANDO. Will you two shut up! This is very legal. Very generous. They pay for the airline tickets...

OLGA. Round trip?

FERNANDO. One way.

OLGA. One way? I see.

FERNANDO. When we get there, to Dallas, to Texas, the congregation will greet us.

OLGA. I am a Catholic! A Catholic. That's the church you married me in!

FERNANDO. They don't want to convert us. There will be a house rented by them, furnished by them.

OLGA. With what they don't want?

FERNANDO. Food in the refrigerator.

OLGA. Charity.

FERNANDO. No. They'll help me find a job, and I'll pay them back.

ROLANDO. Sell the jewelry.

FERNANDO. We promised God never to sell them.

OLGA. Never.

ROLANDO. Listen Fernando, you are flat broke. How much money you got left?

FERNANDO. Seventeen dollars and fifty cents.

ROLANDO. That won't last you more than a week.

OLGA. Longer if we only eat Spam.

ROLANDO. If you sold the jewelry, you could eat steak.

OLGA. When I look into my aquamarine earrings, it's like looking into my grandmother's eyes. She gave me the earrings so I could remember her blue eyes forever.

ROLANDO. Forgive me.

FERNANDO. But our problem is solved –

OLGA. I agreed to come to Miami, then I was told Hialeah, so I agreed to Hialeah. But I am not going farther than 99 miles from my family, from my Cuba.

FERNANDO. But my back? What kind of work can I do with this back?

OLGA. No charity, that's all I ask. I know what it's like to be seen as the poor relative. I have hundreds of them.

ROLANDO. Not me. I never asked your father for anything.

OLGA. No?

ROLANDO. No.

OLGA. I know how people see you, if you accept their crumbs. I remember them. Distant relatives. On Sundays begging for a party. For some chicken and rice. Wearing what did not fit my sister or me anymore. Groveling at our feet. I despised them. Every Sunday. They weren't wanted. They just showed up and we felt we had to give. The worst humiliation in the world. That's charity. That's exile.

FERNANDO. We have to go to Dallas. Meet the Presbyterians. And thank them for their generosity. Please don't make me feel like less than a man.

OLGA. Why did life turn into a tragedy?

FERNANDO. Ah, the pain.

ROLANDO. In your back?

FERNANDO. Yes.

OLGA. I don't know what to do for back pain.

ROLANDO. We have to tie something around it. Put ice on it.

OLGA. I don't have ice.

ROLANDO. You should learn how to make ice cubes.

OLGA. I know how to make ice cubes. My freezer doesn't work!

ROLANDO. I forgot.

OLGA. Go down to your house and get ice.

ROLANDO. Sure. I will. Fine.

(**ROLANDO** *exits.*)

OLGA. Fernando, hold me in your arms and tell me that you were kidding.

FERNANDO. I can't. My back is broken.

OLGA. You are such a baby.

FERNANDO. It was a nightmare, Olga. There are people who spend their entire lives lifting bricks from one part of the stockyard and piling them up on the other side of the stockyard. And other people, like me, who were meant to give those kind of people orders. But I was doing it! I was lifting. I thought this is what I'm doing with my education? Then I pulled a muscle. My back froze. I kept working. But it hurt so much I started weeping.

OLGA. How embarrassing.

FERNANDO. It was.

OLGA. You're such a baby.

FERNANDO. I am great mathematician. I want to make money adding and subtracting, dividing and multiplying. Derivatives and anti-derivatives. Not lifting.

OLGA. I am so scared.

FERNANDO. So am I, Olga.

OLGA. My father told me to marry somebody much older, a mature man that would teach me how to stop being a child. Can we survive here, Fernando?

FERNANDO. We will in Texas.

OLGA. But if we go any further away, how will you fight?

FERNANDO. That's classified information. It has to be.

OLGA. Why can't I join the army?

FERNANDO. Women were not built for combat.

OLGA. How about Joan of Arc?

FERNANDO. You are not Joan of Arc.

OLGA. She believed in her country more than herself. So do I. Can I trust you with our country's future?

FERNANDO. I will do the best I can with our future.

OLGA. Our country's future and our future go hand in hand.

FERNANDO. They asked about our background.

OLGA. The Presbyterians?

FERNANDO. The Texans. They had a questionnaire so they could start looking into possibilities.

OLGA. Possibilities?

FERNANDO. Well, I told them you could sew.

OLGA. I can't sew.

FERNANDO. I am an accountant. I did study at Villanova.

OLGA. I can knit. I can crochet. I can fix a button. But not on one of those machines. Working like a mule.

FERNANDO. You're going to have to.

OLGA. Why didn't we smuggle money out of Cuba, while we still had the chance.

FERNANDO. Our fathers refused to believe that he would take over the country's banks. We didn't have anything of our own, everything belonged to our parents.

OLGA. We lost everything we were going to inherit? Fernando, everything?

FERNANDO. It's all gone.

OLGA. Did we commit some terrible sin? Because I feel like I'm paying. I never noticed people were starving.

FERNANDO. People were not starving.

OLGA. What if they were?

FERNANDO. Then we deserve –

OLGA. This?

FERNANDO. It's not that bad.

OLGA. I keep thinking I'm going to wake up at home, looking out my own window. And that there would be a breeze.

FERNANDO. Pinch yourself. This is real.

(**OLGA** *pinches herself.*)

OLGA. Hialeah?

FERNANDO. Yes, Hialeah.

OLGA. Why?

FERNANDO. Dallas, I hear –

OLGA. It's a desert. It's in the middle of a great American desert. The Mojave.

FERNANDO. No, it's next to Mexico. Texas borders with Mexico, the gulf, and has a very large Spanish population.

(*There is a loud knock on the front door.*)

FERNANDO. Let Rolando in.

OLGA. Why would Rolando knock?

FERNANDO. He's polite.

OLGA. No, he's not, he knows we're waiting for him.

FERNANDO. Open it!

OLGA. You do it.

FERNANDO. My back. I can't!

OLGA. I won't do it. It might be an American.

(*More knocking.*)

FERNANDO. Answer the door, now!

OLGA. What if it's the FBI. Do they know I used to work for Fidel? Do they know I smuggled arms for him and raised money for him by giving canasta parties?

(*More knocking.*)

FERNANDO. Stop it!

OLGA. I'm a traitor everywhere.

FERNANDO. Not in Texas.

OLGA. No, in Texas, I'll only be betraying my God, my church, and my Pope.

FERNANDO. Answer the door God damn it!

(**OLGA** *answers the door.* **ROSITA** *is standing there, holding a suitcase. She is dressed in a Chanel traveling suit.* **OLGA** *slams the door shut.*)

OLGA. Now I'm hallucinating.

ROSITA. Olga, it's been hell. There's nowhere to shop! We've run out of cash! And my hairdresser disappeared in the middle of the night!

(**OLGA** *opens the door.*)

OLGA. It is you.

ROSITA. I'm here!

(**BARBARA** *runs in.*)

BARBARA. Aunt Rosita! I thought I heard you.

(**ROSITA** *and* **BARBARA** *embrace.*)

OLGA. Fernando, it's my sister.

FERNANDO. I'd greet you but I can't move.

ROSITA. Oh?

(**ROSITA** *looks around at the house.*)

ROSITA. Oh my God.

FERNANDO. Welcome to our humble home.

ROSITA. Humble? Excuse me.

(**ROSITA** *runs into the bathroom, we hear her vomiting.*)

BARBARA. Is she drunk?

OLGA. With motherhood. Remember.

BARBARA. But we'll baptize the baby in Cuba.

OLGA. Of course.

FERNANDO. Oh God! The pain just got worse. Where the hell is Rolando?

BARBARA. He got me a costume...

FERNANDO. For Halloween? Good.

OLGA. You approve?

FERNANDO. I told him to get it for her. It's time for her to begin making friends.

OLGA. She has me.

FERNANDO. Children her own age.

OLGA. What will I do?

FERNANDO. You have your sister now.

BARBARA. I gotta go do my homework.

FERNANDO. What homework?

(BARBARA *reads.*)

BARBARA. "My noble father, I do perceive here a divided duty."

OLGA. She's practicing her English.

FERNANDO. Put on your costume.

OLGA. Will she forget her Spanish?

FERNANDO. You'll never let her.

OLGA. That's right. I'll never let her. Never!

FERNANDO. Uh-huh. Barbara put on your costume.

BARBARA. Do I have to?

FERNANDO. Yes! Let her have her dreams.

OLGA. In Spanish.

FERNANDO. In whatever language she wants.

OLGA. Never.

(BARBARA *exits.*)

FERNANDO. Fine. Fine, no happiness till we get back...fine, this could be a great adventure. Now I am going to have to tell the Presbyterians to give me a ticket for your sister.

OLGA. They'll have her?

FERNANDO. Of course. They said the whole family.

OLGA. The whole family is in Cuba.

FERNANDO. Barbara

BARBARA. What?

FERNANDO. Have you put on your costume?

(**BARBARA** *comes out of the bedroom door.*)

BARBARA. I'll face the humiliation when it's necessary. I've got more homework.

FERNANDO. No, put it on now and go out there and enjoy a new holiday.

BARBARA. But my Shakespeare.

FERNANDO. Put it on now.

BARBARA. Fine. Sure. Why not.

(**BARBARA** *exits.*)

FERNANDO. Do you love me?

OLGA. I love my country, Barbara, my parents, you, my sister, my cousins...

FERNANDO. In that order.

OLGA. In that precise order.

(**BARBARA** *enters dressed as a clown.*)

BARBARA. Are you really going to make me go?

OLGA. Go and be part of the "American Dream."

BARBARA. The American Dream?

OLGA. That's what your father insists I'm depriving you of.

FERNANDO. You look wonderful.

OLGA. You look cheap.

FERNANDO. Go.

(**ROSITA** *enters from the bathroom.*)

ROSITA. Goddaughter? Why are you a clown?

BARBARA. The American Dream.

ROSITA. Oh.

FERNANDO. Go. Go have fun.

BARBARA. Where's Uncle Quiko?

ROSITA. He's a coward. He stayed. How's your new school?

BARBARA. I refused to stand up for the pledge of allegiance to their flag.

ROSITA. Good.

BARBARA. It upset my teacher. She took it personally.

ROSITA. It's not your flag. Why should you pledge to it every day?

FERNANDO. Because this country is helping her.

BARBARA. Today she taught us about their revolution against the English monarchs. I told her that our revolution was against the American imperialists. She got very upset when I told her that.

OLGA. Why? You are right.

FERNANDO. Quiet, Olga, people will hear you.

OLGA. Let them. It's the USA's fault that we are not independent.

FERNANDO. Partly their fault, partly Cuba's fault.

ROSITA. I thought it was Spain's fault for keeping us a colony for hundreds of years.

OLGA. Completely Batista's fault. He was the USA's puppet. He did everything they wanted. And you idolized him, Fernando!

FERNANDO. Batista made Cuba rich!

ROSITA. No, we are rich because sugar is valuable.

FERNANDO. And you liked being rich, Olga.

ROSITA. Isn't it?

OLGA. Not at my country's expense.

BARBARA. I think so.

OLGA. Under Batista, Cuba was just a big fat whore! And you know that Fernando!

FERNANDO. Don't you dare say the word "whore!" Not in front of my daughter.

OLGA. I'm sorry, Barbara.

BARBARA. I've heard the word before.

FERNANDO. How can you keep talking against Batista?

OLGA. I cannot believe that you are still defending him.

FERNANDO. He's a lot better than your Fidel Castro.

OLGA. You wanted him, too. You got tired of Batista's interference. You wanted to get rid of American interests on the island. We both went for Fidel.

FERNANDO. That's not true. I pretended to like Fidel to humor you.

ROSITA. I always thought we wanted Fidel because he was so much better looking than Batista.

FERNANDO. I never backed Fidel Castro. Never.

OLGA. How you rewrite history, Fernando.

BARBARA. I am so confused, I idolized Fidel a year ago and now I'm supposed to hate him.

FERNANDO. Every time you are eating Spam instead of lobster remember it is all Fidel Castro's fault.

ROSITA. I think he became a communist because he had no sense of what it feels like to be properly groomed.

BARBARA. I prayed every night for the revolution's victory.

OLGA. I know. I'm sorry. But your father's right. It backfired. The revolution does not work. Remember that, Barbara.

BARBARA. Fine.

FERNANDO. Repeat it.

BARBARA. It backfired. The revolution does not work.

ROSITA. Beautiful. Thank God we got you out of there before the communists brainwashed you.

FERNANDO. Yes, thank God.

(**ROLANDO** *enters*)

ROLANDO. Rosita! Oh my God! My Cousin. I am a happy man. This is a lucky day. How did you get here?

ROSITA. Pan Am.

ROLANDO. Let me hug you.

(**ROLANDO** *hugs* **ROSITA.**)

ROSITA. Sister, what's gotten into him?

OLGA. Nostalgia.

ROLANDO. My family is waiting for you.

OLGA. Your wife is going with them?

ROLANDO. Yes.

ROSITA. Do I have to hug her?

OLGA. No. She never comes in here.

ROSITA. What's gotten into her?

OLGA. She's pretending to be a fallen aristocrat.

ROSITA. Is she? How?

OLGA. By imitating us.

ROLANDO. She's a very complicated person. I'm trying to understand her.

FERNANDO. Go, Barbara, have a real good time.

BARBARA. By the way, the saying is "Trick or Treat," your kids had it all wrong.

ROLANDO. Brat.

OLGA. But you still love her, right?

ROLANDO. Of course, she's my goddaughter.

ROSITA. If your parents ever died, we'd be responsible for you.

ROLANDO. Yes.

BARBARA. Please, Mother, live.

OLGA. I'll try, darling. I'll try.

FERNANDO. Go! Enjoy the holiday.

ROSITA. I'll walk out with you to see the carnival.

*(**ROSITA** and **BARBARA** exit out the front door.)*

OLGA. Sister, stay in front of the house. Don't get lost.

ROLANDO. Here's the ice.

FERNANDO. It's melted.

ROLANDO. Sorry but my wife made me...

FERNANDO. What?

ROLANDO. Wait for her.

FERNANDO. Well I can't use this now.

ROLANDO. Sorry.

FERNANDO. Maybe if I soaked in a hot bath.

ROLANDO. Here's a Valium.

FERNANDO. Thanks.

ROLANDO. Don't I always?

FERNANDO. I'm going to take a shower.

ROLANDO. Hot water on the back.

FERNANDO. Yes.

    (**FERNANDO** *exits.*)

ROLANDO. You know maybe in Texas...

OLGA. I don't want to hear about Texas.

ROLANDO. But Fernando has always been...

OLGA. Keep your opinions to yourself.

ROLANDO. You don't respect me?

OLGA. But I love you. That should be enough.

ROLANDO. How can you not respect me? I've been loyal and I...

OLGA. Because you worked for Batista.

ROLANDO. To advance myself.

OLGA. By being a thug?

ROLANDO. Not everybody had your privileges.

OLGA. And?

ROLANDO. I was not a thug. I was a sergeant.

OLGA. Same thing.

ROLANDO. Fine.

OLGA. Fine.

ROLANDO. Even though you don't respect me. I adore you.

OLGA. Really?

ROLANDO. Yes.

OLGA. Thank you.

ROLANDO. I like it when you ground the Spam and put it into Lima beans. What do you call it?

OLGA. Spam Chili.

ROLANDO. Spam Chili, delicious. I make my wife cook it all the time.

OLGA. Really?

ROLANDO. My wife is jealous.

OLGA. Of me?

ROLANDO. Yes.

OLGA. Because of my cooking?

ROLANDO. No, because you are going to go to Texas. She thinks Fernando is an innovator.

OLGA. Running away is innovation now?

ROLANDO. Yes.

OLGA. She likes it here, doesn't she?

ROLANDO. Yes. She feels like here she's not a victim of a class system. She feels they'll always know she's illegitimate in Cuba, in Guanabacoa.

OLGA. That's true.

ROLANDO. And nobody here has any idea.

OLGA. Don't ever tell your children.

ROLANDO. Of course not.

OLGA. How she ever forgave her mother, I'll never know.

ROLANDO. The one who gives you life is the one who gives you life even if she's a whore.

OLGA. No wonder your wife used to be a kleptomaniac.

ROLANDO. I reformed her. But now...

OLGA. What?

ROLANDO. She blames the church and the nuns for not protecting her mother. This is awful. I shouldn't tell you. I'm ashamed.

OLGA. I'm your cousin.

ROLANDO. I found a "Watchtower"....

OLGA. What?

ROLANDO. In her purse. I go through her purse.

OLGA. What self respecting Cuban man wouldn't?

ROLANDO. She wants to switch religions.

OLGA. You mean your wife is secretly becoming a Jehovah's Witness?

ROLANDO. Yes.

OLGA. My God! Jesus forgive her.

ROLANDO. Amen.

OLGA. See what happens when you leave your country? What will become of us next?

ROLANDO. We'll turn into Jews and murder Jesus.

(*FERNANDO enters.*)

OLGA. What?

FERNANDO. Nothing works here.

OLGA. And?

FERNANDO. The hot water ran out.

ROLANDO. Maybe they'll have plenty of hot water it Texas.

FERNANDO. Maybe.

OLGA. What I really want is my bidet.

ROLANDO. Maybe they'll have bidets in Texas.

FERNANDO. Yes.

OLGA. No.

FERNANDO. Why not?

OLGA. I won't see a bidet again till we attack and liberate our bathroom. Never in this country. Believe me, cleanliness is questionable here.

ROLANDO. You shouldn't talk that way.

OLGA. Why not?

ROLANDO. They can send us back any time they want.

OLGA. No. That's democracy. I can bitch and bitch all I want and they have to accept me because I am proving their system works.

(*ROSITA enters.*)

ROSITA. There's a mob of children running towards the house. What do they want?

OLGA. I don't know.

FERNANDO. Are we supposed to have candy for them?

ROLANDO. Of course. Treats.

OLGA. We don't have any money for treats.

ROSITA. Think of something.

OLGA. Yes, come with me into the kitchen and help me.

ROSITA. I can't cook.

(**OLGA** *goes into kitchen,* **ROSITA** *waits in the hallway.*)

ROSITA. Have you made any flan lately?

OLGA. Can't afford the eggs.

ROSITA. Do you have any bon bons?

(**OLGA** *reenters.*)

OLGA. I'll give them left over Spam.

(*They walk towards the front door.*)

ROSITA. You'll need napkins.

OLGA. Don't have any. You hand them out.

ROSITA. Let's do it together sister.

OLGA. No, I can't.

ROSITA. Why not?

OLGA. I'm not wearing a costume.

ROSITA. Me neither.

OLGA. Please don't make me go out there!

ROSITA. I'll count to three and out the door we'll go. One, two, three.

(**ROSITA** *pushes* **OLGA** *out the door.*)

FERNANDO. Women. Break my back for them and...

ROLANDO. That's better than breaking my balls. Listen, when you got here didn't I have this house waiting?

FERNANDO. Yes. You're a real friend.

ROLANDO. Didn't I arrange it so you could smuggle five hundred dollars through the Swiss Embassy?

FERNANDO. You did.

ROLANDO. You betrayed me.

FERNANDO. Betrayed you? How?

ROLANDO. How could you out-do me in my wife's eyes,

going to Dallas without telling me first?

FERNANDO. My wife hates me because I'm taking her to Dallas.

ROLANDO. And mine is torturing me because I'm not. I guess there's no goddamned way to make a woman happy.

FERNANDO. I guess not.

ROLANDO. What am I gonna do alone here without you?

FERNANDO. Listen, you pioneered for me. I'll pioneer for you.

ROLANDO. You will?

FERNANDO. When I see what Dallas is like, when I get a job, I'll send for you.

ROLANDO. And when I get a job. I'll send for my wife and the kids.

FERNANDO. Of course.

ROLANDO. That makes sense.

FERNANDO. Yes.

ROLANDO. And the struggle?

FERNANDO. When the time comes we will join the brigade and get La Habana back!

ROLANDO. You still want to?

FERNANDO. Yes.

ROLANDO. If we go to Dallas how will we do our basic training?

FERNANDO. In the back yard.

ROLANDO. You sure?

FERNANDO. All we have to do is a lot of sit ups and target practice.

ROLANDO. You're just going to go to Dallas, become a cowboy and forget your past.

FERNANDO. "I am more Cuban than a palm tree. The blood that runs inside of me is a combination of cigar smoke and rum. The only beat I hear in my heart is the rhumba. And I swear on my country, my Cuba, that

I will only dream of holding up your flag and dying for your honor." That's a poem I wrote in High School. I wrote it for the national competition and I still feel that way.

ROLANDO. Forgive me for doubting you. I will be there with you. With machine guns and hand grenades.

FERNANDO. We'll get our revenge.

ROLANDO. Yes. We will.

FERNANDO. Good.

(**OLGA** *and* **ROSITA** *run in.*)

OLGA. We were attacked by a Superman.

ROSITA. And a ghost.

OLGA. They're throwing rotten eggs!

ROSITA. So they hate us for being bourgeois here, too. Or do they think we're Marxist-Leninists?

OLGA. No, it was the Spam.

ROSITA. Lock the door, sister.

OLGA. Oh my God, my daughter is somewhere out there in that mob.

ROLANDO. Don't worry, my wife is with her.

OLGA. Let's hope she hasn't tried to convert her.

ROSITA. What?

ROLANDO. Don't. Please.

OLGA. He's trying to keep his wife from...

ROSITA. Have you been fooling around again?

ROLANDO. No, my wife has.

FERNANDO. Oh my god. Rolando. You should have told me.

ROLANDO. With Jehovah!

FERNANDO. Slap her around a couple of times and tell her to forget him!

OLGA. Jehovah is another word for God.

FERNANDO. What?

OLGA. She's been fooling around with religion. With

different kinds of religion.

ROSITA. She's becoming a Jehovah's Witness?

ROLANDO. I've got to respect her. She's very complicated.

ROSITA. Why you ever married her we will never know.

ROLANDO. I loved her, she needed my protection...

ROSITA. And our family name!

ROLANDO. Don't talk about my wife like that. How about your husband?

ROSITA. What about my husband?

ROLANDO. Everyone knows that he...

FERNANDO. So, Rosita is having a baby.

ROLANDO. With him?

OLGA. Of course.

ROSITA. What a surprise, huh?

OLGA. I was surprised.

ROLANDO. You knew about this?

OLGA. Yes of course, she tells me everything. She's my sister.

ROLANDO. Everyone knew, and no one was going to tell me.

OLGA. I didn't think you cared.

ROLANDO. I care about my family.

OLGA. I thought if Rosita wanted you to know, she'd write you a letter.

ROLANDO. Why didn't you write me?

ROSITA. I didn't think you cared about things like that.

ROLANDO. Well I do!

ROSITA. Had they censored it? Had they opened it?

OLGA. What?

ROSITA. My letter.

OLGA. Yes. Someone wrote, "P.S. Congratulate Rosita for us."

ROSITA. That stupid block committee. I hate them. Our whole block knows I'm pregnant.

ROLANDO. Before your cousin.

ROSITA. Did you recognize the handwriting?

OLGA. Marta, yes.

ROSITA. Even our next door neighbor betrayed us. No one knows what it is like. Leaving, going. They have a fish tank now.

ROLANDO. Tropical fish?

ROSITA. No, a glass enclosure. When you are leaving they sit you there.

OLGA. Before you go?

ROSITA. Yes, at the airport. I sat there for ten hours.

ROLANDO. Bastards.

ROSITA. I felt like a cockroach. Does this place have cockroaches?

ROLANDO. Well...

OLGA. Yes.

FERNANDO. But they don't have cockroaches in the desert.

ROLANDO. Is that where Dallas is, in the desert?

OLGA. It's the armpit of the world.

ROSITA. It was the most degrading experience of my life.

OLGA. Sister?

ROSITA. You're the fish and they watch you.

OLGA. The Milicianos?

ROSITA. And your relatives. It was suffocating.

ROLANDO. No air conditioning?

ROSITA. No. Then on the other side of the glass were Mama and Papa...my husband. He started to cry. His mother held him in her overprotective fat arms. He finally came over to the glass, gestured that I should give him a kiss. I gestured, "no"...he fainted, his mother cursed me. She pounded on the glass. Mama and Papa walked away. He came to and started crying again...oh God, that family can make scenes. It made the Milicianos notice me...and they searched me everywhere, sister, everywhere...Do you understand?

OLGA. Yes. I do.

ROSITA. They made me hand everything over. They took my gold rosary. Why? I thought they did not believe in being Catholics.

OLGA. They believe in gold.

ROLANDO. Sons of bitches.

ROSITA. But the terrible thing is, Olga, I didn't just hate the Milicianos.

OLGA. No?

ROSITA. I also hated my husband and his mother for thinking they were the ones suffering. I wanted to get out! I wanted to scream! But I kept my dignity. I was dying... my breath stopped...I needed air...I just wanted to go home. Home.

(**ROSITA** *starts to cry.*)

ROLANDO. Cousin.

(**ROLANDO** *touches* **ROSITA***'s hands.*)

ROLANDO. I'm so sorry, cousin.

FERNANDO. Well. Now you're here and you're free to cry.

OLGA. Big deal.

FERNANDO. It is.

OLGA. Go...

FERNANDO. Why?

OLGA. I'm sure she'd like a Coca Cola.

FERNANDO. We are on a budget.

ROLANDO. I got a couple of dollars. I'll buy rum. Rum and coke, cousin. You'd like that?

ROSITA. Thank you.

FERNANDO. Don't worry, you'll give birth to an American and he will live in liberty.

OLGA. That baby is going to be born in Cuba.

ROLANDO. Of course.

OLGA. Go buy the rum and coke. Steal some limes from the house on the corner. And we'll give my sister a

"Cuba Libre."

ROLANDO. Okay.

FERNANDO. I'll go with you.

(**ROLANDO** *and* **FERNANDO** *exit.*)

ROSITA. What do you do all day here?

OLGA. We sit, we wait. That's what I've been doing for the last three months. Sitting, waiting...missing my life... trying to put up a good front, failing at it. Enjoying nothing.

ROSITA. This place is dreary.

OLGA. Like a tomb.

(*We hear pounding on the doors. Children screaming, "Trick or treat." A rotten egg hits the window.* **ROSITA** *is terrified.* **OLGA** *goes to the door. She screams.*)

OLGA. Yankee go home!

ROSITA. Olga, no!

OLGA. Yankee go home!

(*We hear the children leaving.*)

ROSITA. Why are they doing this?

OLGA. They hate us.

ROSITA. But why?

OLGA. Propaganda. Everybody wants someone to hate. Who better than us? People who ran away from their own country. Cowards.

ROSITA. We are worms, aren't we?

OLGA. They think we are spies, or after their jobs. Or traitors to the greatest revolution since their own. Depends on what side of the political spectrum they sit. Some of them idolize Fidel.

ROSITA. But he hates this country. You should hear him lately.

OLGA. They feel guilty because of their wealth.

ROSITA. Thank God we never felt like that.

(*There is pounding on the kitchen window.*)

OLGA. Not another attack!

(**OLGA** *and* **ROSITA** *drop to the floor.*)

BARBARA (O.S.) Let me in! Please let me in!

ROSITA. It's my niece. I hear my niece's voice.

OLGA. Barbara, where are you?

BARBARA (O.S.) By the kitchen!

OLGA. What's wrong.

BARBARA (O.S.) Someone is following me. Unlock the window!

(**OLGA** *walks towards the kitchen.*)

OLGA. Always keep your windows locked in this country.

ROSITA. Really?

(**OLGA** *and* **BARBARA** *walk in.* **BARBARA***'s costume is torn. Her mask looks as if someone had stepped on it. She takes it off.*)

OLGA. Oh Jesus. Sweet Jesus!

ROSITA. You are right, they hate us!

OLGA. Oh my darling. And your father made me bring you here to protect you.

BARBARA. I hate men!

OLGA. Men did this to you. Aaaah!

ROSITA. Calm down. It was boys. Boys beat you up, right?

BARBARA. Yes.

OLGA. Thank you, God the father, the Son, and the Holy Ghost, Amen!

BARBARA. Where is he?

ROSITA. They went to the store.

BARBARA. I hate him so much.

OLGA. Are you hating your father again?

BARBARA. No.

OLGA. Good. It's a sin to hate your father.

ROSITA. A terrible sin. One of the worst.

BARBARA. My godfather. I hate my godfather!

OLGA. I don't know if that's a sin or not?

ROSITA. Must be. Don't you think?

OLGA. I'll ask Father Beneficio.

ROSITA. He's here?

OLGA. Right in Hialeah.

ROSITA. But he won't be in Dallas.

BARBARA. Dallas?

ROSITA. That's where we are going to live.

OLGA. Maybe.

BARBARA. And you weren't going to tell me?

OLGA. It's your father's idea.

BARBARA. You promised after Cuba. You promised.

ROSITA. What?

OLGA. To tell her what we are planning.

(**BARBARA** *has covered her face with her hands.*)

OLGA. Remember, only Jesus is perfect.

(**BARBARA** *does not respond.*)

OLGA. That usually works.

ROSITA. She's really upset.

(**FERNANDO** *and* **ROLANDO** *enter.*)

ROLANDO. A toast, we are going to have a toast.

ROSITA. I need one.

FERNANDO. What happened to the window?

OLGA. The natives.

ROLANDO. You should have bought a bag of candy, Fernando.

FERNANDO. With what?

ROLANDO. A loan from me.

OLGA. It's not our holiday.

ROLANDO. When in Rome do as the Romans do.

OLGA. They may have conquered you. But they have not conquered me.

ROLANDO. Why is everything political with you?

OLGA. Because politics have ruined my life.

ROSITA. Don't depress me, please.

FERNANDO. Negativity, that's your sister.

(**ROLANDO** *goes up to* **BARBARA.**)

ROLANDO. Why aren't you out with my wife?

BARBARA. You! You putrid piece of shit!

OLGA. She spoke!

FERNANDO. Don't you dare speak to a man like that!

BARBARA. The kids started calling me a communist. They made fun of my accent, followed me everywhere I went. I had to go out and beg for candy. This is what you want me to become a part of, Papi? This?

ROLANDO. My children, my poor children. What did they do to them?

BARBARA. Nothing.

ROLANDO. They ran?

OLGA. Fast, like their father.

FERNANDO. That's the trouble with you, sweetheart. You always want to fight like your mother.

BARBARA. His children joined in.

ROLANDO. I don't believe you.

BARBARA. Well, they did. They don't care. They yelled, "Communist!"

ROLANDO. It's their mother. She spends all day handing out "Watchtowers."

BARBARA. I'm going to bed.

OLGA. I'll start the shower.

BARBARA. No. I want to sleep with this on me. So I don't forget.

FERNANDO. Not in my room. If you want to sleep in my room, you take a shower.

OLGA. Fernando, you have to sleep on the couch tonight.

FERNANDO. Why?

OLGA. My sister, my daughter and I will share the two

beds.

BARBARA. The women.

ROSITA. I can sleep on the couch.

OLGA. No, you're pregnant.

BARBARA. Good night

FERNANDO. Wait a minute.

OLGA. Leave her alone.

FERNANDO. I don't want her to sleep with defeat on her mind. Go out there and...

BARBARA. No!

FERNANDO. Go back out there and face them and ask for candy.

BARBARA. Never.

OLGA. I won't let her.

BARBARA. They despise me.

FERNANDO. Come here.

OLGA. Leave her alone.

ROSITA. Please, Fernando.

FERNANDO. What did you do to those kids?

BARBARA. Nothing. I'm going to bed.

FERNANDO. Answer me!

OLGA. She'll tell you about it tomorrow, when it's not so painful anymore.

BARBARA. I shared a confidence with his kids and they betrayed me.

OLGA. Figures.

FERNANDO. What did you say?

BARBARA. That I'm not going to ask a bunch of white trash for candy.

FERNANDO. I thought so? See?

BARBARA. I didn't bother anyone.

FERNANDO. No one is going to like her, Olga.

OLGA. Plenty of Cubans like her.

FERNANDO. But I want people here to like her.

OLGA. But I don't.

BARBARA. I am not going out and that's that!

ROSITA. Please, no more fighting. It's my first night here.

FERNANDO. Sorry.

OLGA. You're right.

FERNANDO. Go to bed, Barbara.

BARBARA. I'm sorry I disappointed you.

FERNANDO. I'll get over it.

BARBARA. Next holiday, I'll try to do whatever is called for.

FERNANDO. Thank you, Barbara.

ROLANDO. All you have to do in the next one is eat turkey.

OLGA. She hates turkey.

ROLANDO. You can also eat pumpkin pie.

BARBARA. I'll try to eat that.

ROLANDO. Barbara, will you ever forgive me?

BARBARA. I don't know. I'll never forgive your children. Is it alright to hate them?

OLGA. Yes.

FERNANDO. For Christ sake, Olga, you encourage her.

OLGA. They're fourth cousins. They don't count.

BARBARA. Good night.

(**BARBARA** *exits.*)

ROSITA. It's all going round and round in my head. Good-bye, hello. Is there a time change?

FERNANDO. It's only ninety miles away.

ROSITA. So near and yet so far. Is that a song? I'll sing her that song she liked when she was a little girl.

(**ROSITA** *exits.*)

ROLANDO. I can never go home again.

OLGA. Your kids would do great in Cuba working for the Block Committees, ratting on people.

ROLANDO. I have to get drunk before I can face her. Let me make myself a drink.

OLGA. Remember, no ice.

ROLANDO. Then three Cuba Libres, straight?

FERNANDO. Count me in.

ROLANDO. Please, cousin.

OLGA. Alright. But only because of the name.

ROLANDO. Maybe I'll ask Barbara if she wants...

BARBARA (O.S.) I don't want any, thank you.

ROLANDO. She wants nothing from me.

FERNANDO. She'll get over it.

OLGA. When you die, she'll forgive you.

BARBARA (O.S.) Maybe.

ROLANDO. In America they call this drink Rum and Coke.

OLGA. If you want to drink it at my house you better call it, "Cuba Libre"!

ROLANDO. In Dallas you'll be the only Cubans, rare.

(**ROLANDO** *starts to mix the drinks*)

FERNANDO. Yes, and slowly we will melt into the pot.

ROLANDO. Into the U.S.A. Melting Pot?

FERNANDO. That's right.

OLGA. Like ice cubes?

FERNANDO. Yes, like ice cubes.

OLGA. Ice cubes have to freeze before they can melt.

FERNANDO. What do you mean?

OLGA. Change form.

(**ROSITA** *rushes back in.*)

ROSITA. I need a drink.

FERNANDO. What's wrong?

ROSITA. Barbara is scaring me. She thinks this Dallas trip is all a plot of the CIA...to get the Cubans out of Miami. She says if we go there no one will be waiting for us. And we will all be begging on the streets, like she was tonight.

FERNANDO. She has a very vivid imagination.

ROLANDO. She could be right.

FERNANDO. No.

ROLANDO. Here are the drinks. Who's gonna do the toast?

ROSITA. I will. Columbus sailed the seven seas. To find what no one else could see. And then one day by accident his boat hit land and it was Cuba. Cristobal, dear, you were lucky. If you sailed just ninety miles to the north, this is where you'd be. And it is dreary here. Believe me.

ROLANDO. That's not a toast.

ROSITA. I tried.

ROLANDO. You do it, Olga.

(**OLGA** *raises her glass.*)

ROSITA. Yes, go ahead sister.

OLGA. We are going to do everything we can to get our country back! Even if it takes the rest of our lives. We love La Habana, it was our town. We were born there. My daughter was born there. My grandparents are buried there. I left behind my wedding pictures, my bedroom furniture, my favorite restaurant. Barbara's first drawings, my rose garden, my diaries, my cookbooks and diplomas. My friends, my aunts and uncles, my cousins, my mother and my father. My childhood. My language. My past, my future. Everything.

FERNANDO. Olga. I swear to you.

OLGA. Cuba Libre?

FERNANDO. Cuba Libre!

ALL. Cuba Libre!

(*They all begin to toast. The phone rings.* **FERNANDO** *answers.*)

FERNANDO. Alo? Yes...we will be ready to go. In a week?

(*Blackout*)

ACT TWO

Dallas, Texas. A month later. Late afternoon. A ranch house. A family room and kitchen. Nothing in the house matches. There are curtains of all different colors in front of a set of French doors, different sized chairs around a dinette table. This was a place that was put together with a lot of donations, things that other people did not want: out of style but in many ways fanciful. **BARBARA** *is reading through the newspaper.* **ROSITA** *is having a Coca-cola to help her morning sickness. We hear a car pull up,* **FERNANDO** *walks in.*

BARBARA. "The Parent Trap" is still playing. Can we go?

FERNANDO. What's that?

BARBARA. The movie the Presbyterians took us to.

ROSITA. I didn't get the jokes in that movie.

BARBARA. I did.

FERNANDO. Good.

BARBARA. They're identical twins. People can't tell them apart, so they switch identities, they live in two worlds. Can we go?

FERNANDO. That's what you like about it?

BARBARA. Yes. They're like us.

ROSITA. That's true. It's played by the same actress.

FERNANDO. What do you mean by that?

ROSITA. That Haley Mills plays...

FERNANDO. No, I'm talking to Barbara.

BARBARA. You know.

FERNANDO. No, tell me.

BARBARA. We are stuck between two worlds.

FERNANDO. I'm not.

BARBARA. You're not?

FERNANDO. No.

BARBARA. Really?

FERNANDO. No, I am still me. In whatever country, I am myself.

BARBARA. Wow! So can we go?

FERNANDO. We'll see.

ROSITA. That simple?

FERNANDO. That simple.

ROSITA. Don't let my sister hear you say that.

FERNANDO. Someday she'll have to understand.

BARBARA. We are going back in a few months. It won't make a difference then.

ROSITA. Right.

FERNANDO. She's still at work?

ROSITA. "Over-time."

FERNANDO. Good. She is trying hard.

BARBARA. What's that mean? Over-time?

ROSITA. When you work past the regular hours. If I didn't have morning sickness all day long, I'd be there also.

FERNANDO. I'm sure you would be.

ROSITA. You bet.

BARBARA. Mama said that with her next paycheck she would buy something that matched. Even if it was just a set of kitchen towels.

FERNANDO. Why?

BARBARA. Look around, nothing matches here. In Cuba everything...

FERNANDO. Can I tell you something, Barbara? In our perfectly matched, manicured environment back there, back home in El Vedado.

BARBARA. Yes, Papi?

FERNANDO. Underneath it, everything was either chaotic or oppressive.

ROSITA. That's true. We were always under somebody's thumb.

FERNANDO. That's why we were fooled into a revolution. Here in Dallas, Texas, we're free!

BARBARA. Free?

FERNANDO. Yes!

ROSITA. That's true. It feels good.

FERNANDO. It does. Doesn't it?

ROSITA. To not be society anymore.

FERNANDO. Yes!

ROSITA. Don't tell Olga.

FERNANDO. She'll find out for herself.

ROSITA. At some point, I hope.

FERNANDO. She's thinking of letting me put the jewelry into a safe deposit box.

ROSITA. Thinking and doing are two different things.

FERNANDO. If she can get rid of her jewels, she can get rid of her past.

ROSITA. We'll see.

BARBARA. She's only considering that because she is afraid the Presbyterians would want to borrow them.

FERNANDO. What?

BARBARA. They are always staring at them.

FERNANDO. They're not used to it.

BARBARA. Last Sunday at church. They kept looking at her emerald crucifix and the keep away the evil eye black ball.

FERNANDO. They wouldn't be caught dead with a crucifix.

BARBARA. But a diamond bracelet fits any religion.

FERNANDO. Especially in Texas.

ROSITA. There was a time when we wouldn't be caught dead at a Presbyterian Church.

FERNANDO. It would be wrong not to go.

ROSITA. They're not trying to convert us, are they?

FERNANDO. Absolutely not.

BARBARA. They think we already are.

ROSITA. Presbyterian?

FERNANDO. No.

ROSITA. They just want to help us, right?

FERNANDO. Yep. Partner they shore do!

BARBARA. Are you a cowboy now, Daddy?

FERNANDO. I'm trying.

(**OLGA** *walks in. She is wearing work clothes. She looks tired and disheveled.*)

ROSITA. Sister you are back early.

OLGA. Yes I am... I am never going back there.

FERNANDO. Of course you're going back.

OLGA. Really? I wasn't brought up for this kind of work, Fernando.

FERNANDO. We are in America now.

OLGA. I am not an American.

ROSITA. Were the Mexicans making fun of you again? I don't know why they're mean to you and nice to me.

OLGA. They think you are an unwed mother, like one of them.

ROSITA. You have to learn to like them. You should eat one of their burritos like I do.

OLGA. I don't like re-fried beans.

FERNANDO. Why not?

OLGA. Because I like Chinese, Spanish, French, Italian, or Cuban food. But not Mexican.

FERNANDO. Why not try!

OLGA. I don't know how.

FERNANDO. You are so stubborn.

OLGA. Am I?

BARBARA. Mama, your hand is bleeding.

OLGA. Yes it is.

ROSITA. Sister?

FERNANDO. Olga?

OLGA. I was on the machine and it...I...I stuck a needle through my finger.

FERNANDO. Oh my God.

OLGA. Single needle machine.

FERNANDO. It pierced you?

OLGA. Like a knife.

(**OLGA** *starts to cry.*)

BARBARA. Mama?

ROSITA. Let me see it, sister. Please.

FERNANDO. Oh God. Olga...

OLGA. It hurt. God, Fernando, it hurt.

ROSITA. It's still bleeding.

FERNANDO. Let me see.

OLGA. It went through the finger nail...

BARBARA. We have to bandage it.

FERNANDO. Yes.

BARBARA. We don't have a first aid kit.

FERNANDO. I'll go next door.

OLGA. To the Presbyterian?

FERNANDO. Of course.

OLGA. No. She'll come over.

FERNANDO. She's nice.

OLGA. She looks at me like I am from another planet.

FERNANDO. To her you are.

OLGA. Catholic is another planet to her.

FERNANDO. We have to bandage your finger.

OLGA. No, stay.

FERNANDO. I'll go to the store and get bandages.

OLGA. Don't run away.

FERNANDO. I'll be right back. I promise.

OLGA. Don't ask them for help.

FERNANDO. I'll buy it at the supermarket.

(**FERNANDO** *leaves. We hear his car drive away.*)

OLGA. Is he sorry?

ROSITA. Of course.

OLGA. Yes, of course.

ROSITA. Did it bleed all over the place?

OLGA. Like an oil well, all over the machine, the swim suits...I was doing fine. They had me on the single needle machine doing the operation where you place the label on the swim suit...in the back. Always in the back, labels. I was getting faster, my mind drifted. I started thinking about the nuns, Rosita. About the convent school, about their Saturday lunches, how we all sat with our white lace veils, our embroidered dresses. Remember?

ROSITA. Yes. They made the best flan.

OLGA. I started feeling the sun, the Caribbean sun, how we protected ourselves from its heat, sitting in the shade of the magnolia trees, always staying white. Then needle... Needle...the single needle machine. I froze. I screamed. I screamed in Spanish. But no one came.

ROSITA. That's terrible.

OLGA. So I pulled it out myself. Never forget Cuba, Barbara. That's all that matters. Remember who you are.

BARBARA. I do.

OLGA. Whenever we start to forget we must prick our fingers till we bleed.

ROSITA. Like an offering?

BARBARA. No, like a sacrifice.

OLGA. That's right.

BARBARA. I like that.

OLGA. When ever I look at this finger again, I'll remember the Caribbean sun. It's my own stigmata. Pain will always make us remember who we are. Where we belong. And it's not here, we must never belong here.

ROSITA. You don't think so?

OLGA. We're Cubans. We can only belong there.

BARBARA. Our own stigmata. I like that. I'll do it! I'll go get a sewing needle.

(**BARBARA** *exits.*)

ROSITA. Make ourselves bleed?

OLGA. Yes.

ROSITA. To remember?

OLGA. We have to.

ROSITA. Are you sure this is rational?

OLGA. Sacrifices don't have to be rational.

ROSITA. So this is going to be our sacrifice?

OLGA. Yes. Until we get home.

ROSITA. Once a week or what?

OLGA. When ever we need it. Once a month.

ROSITA. Will you do it for me? Bring us closer together. You know what a coward I am. You know I admire you.

OLGA. I'd love to.

(OLGA *undoes the bandage.* ROSITA *looks at* OLGA*'s hand.*)

ROSITA. Sister. Your hands have lost...

OLGA. They look like somebody else's hands, don't they?

ROSITA. They're bruised.

OLGA. From the machine. I had to cut my nails. Or they would break.

ROSITA. I guess ironing is an easier job.

OLGA. Nothing is easy on an assembly line.

ROSITA. My hands are still beautiful, aren't they?

OLGA. Yes. You haven't been there enough.

ROSITA. I have morning sickness.

OLGA. I know.

(BARBARA *runs back in with a needle.*)

BARBARA. Here it is! Here I go! I want to really bleed!

(*She pricks herself.*)

BARBARA. It's all coming back. Varadero, 1958. Christmas Eve, oh God. When I had the flu and Daddy caught a swordfish... The smell of the suppository. Swordfish and a penicillin suppository, is that all I can remember?

OLGA. My turn.

(*She pins herself.*)

OLGA. Oh yes. God yes... Oh...

ROSITA. What? What!

OLGA. Sunrise in my own bed, a breeze, covering my body, the smell of gardenias...yes.

BARBARA. I wanna do it again. I think I'll get a better memory. I'm feeling lucky.

ROSITA. No!

OLGA. Sure.

ROSITA. She can't prick herself every time she feels lucky. She'll develop masochistic behavior in a country that thrives on it.

(**BARBARA** *takes the pin and pricks herself.*)

BARBARA. My first communion, my beautiful white dress, God entering my body, white roses...oh yes. Thank you...

ROSITA. Do me! Do me! I want to remember a day of shopping.

OLGA. Barbara get me a match. You're pregnant. It can't have any germs.

(*She sterilizes the sewing needle then is about to pin* **ROSITA.***)*

ROSITA. Wait. I'm already remembering....the greatest department store in the world...you get there by...it's on the corner of...

OLGA. Sister if you've forgotten where to go shopping you're in trouble.

ROSITA. No. Don't prick me. El Encanto is at the corner of Galiano and San Rafael... I have to close my eyes.

OLGA. Promise me sister, you won't give birth till you're back home. You'll hold onto that baby till we liberate La Habana. Nobody in our family is going to be an American, right?

(**ROSITA** *nods yes.* **OLGA** *pricks her.*)

ROSITA. Ay! Yes! I've just spent five hundred dollars on a dress.

BARBARA. What color?

ROSITA. Aqua.

BARBARA. How delicious.

(FERNANDO is there.)

FERNANDO. What are you doing?

BARBARA. A ritual.

FERNANDO. What kind?

ROSITA. Something the nuns taught us years ago.

OLGA. Women's business.

BARBARA. Blood and...pain and recollection...

FERNANDO. Never mind, I don't need to know.

OLGA. Actually you do. We were trying to remember who we were.

FERNANDO. Really? You've forgotten.

OLGA. Sometimes.

FERNANDO. You are my wife. Let me bandage your finger.

(He starts to bandage her finger.)

OLGA. Look at me. I go to the factory. I come home. I'm afraid of getting lost on the bus. It's too cold for me. I'm not used to it. I have never worn a winter coat. My skin is drying from the gas heater. That's never happened to me. I can't understand what anyone is saying to me. I have no friends. My hands are bruised. I want my home. My home.

FERNANDO. You are brave.

OLGA. Do not flatter me.

FERNANDO. I'm sorry.

OLGA. About what?

FERNANDO. Making you work.

OLGA. Our fate.

FERNANDO. No.

OLGA. No?

FERNANDO. You don't have to go back.

OLGA. Why?

FERNANDO. I want you to be happy.

OLGA. I thought...

FERNANDO. It will just take us a little longer to pay the Presbyterians back. But...

OLGA. Are you sure?

FERNANDO. I'm here to protect you. Done.

(**OLGA** *looks at her bandaged finger.*)

OLGA. Crippled.

BARBARA. You'll be here when I get home from school, Mama.

OLGA. We'll see.

FERNANDO. Yes, she will and when I get home from work.

(*They kiss.*)

ROSITA. But I'm going back to work.

FERNANDO. Yes you are.

ROSITA. I want to establish my own identity.

OLGA. What? Unwed mother?

ROSITA. Sure, why not. Better than married to a Mama's boy.

OLGA. True.

FERNANDO. Done.

BARBARA. You're going to stay home with me. Say that you are.

OLGA. I don't know.

BARBARA. Why? It's lonely without you.

OLGA. I know. I miss Hialeah. There were more Cubans there.

BARBARA. Here we are the only Cubans. They have never seen a Cuban before. They think we are Mexicans.

FERNANDO. No they don't.

BARBARA. Yes they do.

ROSITA. Impossible.

OLGA. I miss Rolando. Who ever thought that I would miss Rolando?

(**FERNANDO** *gets up, goes to the grocery bag, and brings out a steak.*)

FERNANDO. I bought us a steak.

ROSITA. A steak, oh my God. No more tuna casserole!

BARBARA. I like tuna.

FERNANDO. Olga?

OLGA. I think we should all learn new things.

FERNANDO. What?

OLGA. We're in America now.

FERNANDO. Okay. Of course. Rosita?

ROSITA. Yes.

FERNANDO. You ready?

ROSITA. I shouldn't cook it.

OLGA. Do it sister, "Cook" could be part of your new identity.

FERNANDO. I'll help you.

ROSITA. Thank you. How do I start?

OLGA. Go into the kitchen.

ROSITA. Right.

FERNANDO. Yes.

OLGA. Neither of you have set foot in the kitchen since we moved here.

FERNANDO. That's not true. I put the groceries away.

BARBARA. Once.

OLGA. Bravo.

(**FERNANDO** *and* **ROSITA** *walk into the kitchen area.*)

ROSITA. Olga, how do I start?

OLGA. You need lemons and garlic and onions, salt and pepper, oil.

FERNANDO. Onions, oil.

ROSITA. Onions and garlic. I'll find the garlic.

FERNANDO. And lemons.

ROSITA. And lemons.

> (**OLGA** *walks towards the windows. She leans her face against the window.*)

OLGA. This glass feels so cold.

FERNANDO. This is as cold as it gets.

> (**ROSITA** *looks through shelves.*)

ROSITA. Jello, a lot of Jello, powdered mashed potatoes. Evaporated milk, canned peas. Oh my God! A can of Spam!

> (*They throw the Spam can around and toss it out the window.*)

ROSITA. It's nice to laugh.

BARBARA. I gotta see the news.

ROSITA. Why?

BARBARA. The weather, there might be a bigger cold front coming.

FERNANDO. So?

BARBARA. I had a dream last night. I heard the head nun's voice from my school, the one that died. She said when ice falls from the sky it means hope is on its way.

FERNANDO. Then let's hope it snows.

BARBARA. That would be a miracle.

FERNANDO. Yes. We have a whole winter. Winter.

ROSITA. Such a new thing.

> (**BARBARA** *goes.* **ROSITA** *is at the stove.*)

ROSITA. Sister, how do I turn that on?

> (**FERNANDO** *goes over to the stove.*)

FERNANDO. Let me see, hmmm. I once used an electric one. It had buttons.

OLGA. You two wouldn't be able to feed yourselves if –

FERNANDO. That's why I married you.

ROSITA. I'm willing to learn.

OLGA. I'll cook it.

FERNANDO. You're sure?

OLGA. It relaxes me. We have an electric skillet for frying. These are much better.

(**OLGA** *starts to cut the onions and garlic.*)

ROSITA. Why?

OLGA. They heat up faster.

FERNANDO. As fast as you can make it. I am starving.

ROSITA. I think in the end it paid off.

OLGA. What?

ROSITA. All the times you spent in the kitchen with the cooks.

(**OLGA** *starts to fry the steak, garlic and onions.*)

OLGA. I didn't learn to cook from them. I learned to cook at finishing school.

ROSITA. And how to re-cane chairs.

OLGA. Things to do with your hands.

(**OLGA** *cuts a lemon and pours the juice over the steak.*)

FERNANDO. What a beautiful sight.

OLGA. The steak?

FERNANDO. You!

ROSITA. I guess it's time for the weather.

OLGA. Don't you want to learn how to cook?

ROSITA. Later.

FERNANDO. Thank you.

ROSITA. Three's a crowd.

(**ROSITA** *goes.*)

FERNANDO. You know the Texans actually think a wife should stay at home with the kids.

OLGA. A Presbyterian wife.

FERNANDO. What?

OLGA. You told them that we are Presbyterians.

FERNANDO. How do you know?

OLGA. I can tell.

FERNANDO. So what, they're helping us...

OLGA. We are lying to them. I am Catholic...

FERNANDO. Pretending...Not lying.

OLGA. To be immigrants?

FERNANDO. Maybe.

OLGA. I'm an exile, not an immigrant.

FERNANDO. But if you were a little bit less arrogant.

OLGA. I'm not arrogant. I'm proud.

FERNANDO. Your jewelry gives you away.

OLGA. My father worked very hard so I could be proud.

FERNANDO. Your father is not here anymore. Let me protect you.

OLGA. I don't trust you. You lied about our religion, you want to be here. An exile is a person who is waiting to go back home!

FERNANDO. So I lied. I was scared, Olga. When we got on the plane from Miami to come here we only had twelve dollars left. What would I have done if nobody was here waiting for us? But they were and they got us jobs. Like they promised. And they got us this house like they said. And I can protect the three of you, the most precious gems I have. I bought us a steak. I earned the money myself. I am so grateful for all this. All of this is ours. Help us survive.

OLGA. I'll try to be strong.

FERNANDO. Thank you, Olga.

(*OLGA goes.*)

Is the steak burning?

(*OLGA comes back in with the bag of jewelry.*)

OLGA. Here. Put them away. In a safe deposit box.

(*She hands him the bag, and removes the rest from her body.*)

OLGA. My cross, my keep away the evil eye black ball, my engagement ring.

FERNANDO. Thank you.

OLGA. I'm sure Rosita will give you hers. She wants to be somebody else. And I will stay home.

FERNANDO. You won't be sorry. Remember, rare.

OLGA. Right.

FERNANDO. There's something that's as good here as at home.

OLGA. Tell me.

FERNANDO. You and me.

OLGA. Yes.

FERNANDO. You and me together, knowing where to touch from all these years of being with each other. That's home.

OLGA. Marriage.

FERNANDO. Family.

OLGA. Yes.

FERNANDO. That's not exile. Don't overcook the steak.

OLGA. It's done.

(She places the steak in front of him.)

FERNANDO. Perfect.

*(**OLGA** cuts a piece of meat and holds it up.)*

FERNANDO. You're going to feed me?

OLGA. Yes I am.

FERNANDO. Good.

*(**OLGA** feeds him.)*

OLGA. You like it?

FERNANDO. Just like home.

OLGA. Please, Fernando. Promise me that you'll fight to get our country back?

FERNANDO. I swear on my mother's...

OLGA. Not on your mother. Swear on the strength of our marriage.

FERNANDO. On my devotion towards you. I swear I'll get you back the thing you want the most.

OLGA. Thank you.

FERNANDO. And you'll be a good Presbyterian wife?

OLGA. Yes. That will be my disguise. Till we get home.

FERNANDO. When it's time for me to fight. I will fight.

OLGA. I love you.

(She kisses him.)

OLGA. We have our own room now.

(He kisses her.)

OLGA. You taste like Cuba.

(Transition.)

ACT THREE

April, 1961. The living room. There are candles placed everywhere. A record player and a television set. Couches and end tables. A lot of knickknacks from the forties.

BARBARA *runs in dressed in a Catholic school uniform. She is practicing her Shakespeare.*

BARBARA. "My noble father I do perceive here a divided duty...My noble father I do perceive here a divided duty... To you I am bound for life and education..."

*(***ROLANDO** *enters from the kitchen.)*

ROLANDO. What are you doing?

BARBARA. Desdemona.

ROSITA (O.S.) Rolando, help!

ROLANDO. Her beans must be burning again.

BARBARA. Must be.

*(***ROLANDO** *walks back in into the kitchen.)*

BARBARA. To you I am bound for life and education...

*(***ROSITA** *walks in. She is now nine months pregnant and is dressed in a loud maternity outfit that she inherited from a Texan. She is carrying a white dress.)*

ROSITA. Please put it on.

BARBARA. No.

ROSITA. I told you to put it on an hour ago.

BARBARA. No, it's a second hand wedding dress.

ROSITA. That's the closest to coming out they had in Texas.

BARBARA. I'll wait till we are all back in Cuba.

ROSITA. You're going to ruin your sweet fifteen.

BARBARA. Why is everybody always trying to dress me?

ROSITA. 'Cause we love you. Now put this on.

BARBARA. I don't want to!

ROSITA. Your mother and I spent two days searching for it. So you could have a nice dress.

BARBARA. But tonight it'll be over. After they finish with the communists at "The Bay Of Pigs."

ROSITA. Shh! Don't talk too loudly about it.

BARBARA. Why?

ROSITA. Fidel has spies everywhere.

BARBARA. But they already announced the invasion on the news. They said last night an invasion had begun.

ROSITA. Right. Sorry.

BARBARA. That's why we are having a party.

ROSITA. That's true.

BARBARA. Yes it is.

ROSITA. Here is your father with the cake.

BARBARA. I hate American cakes. They're dry and the frosting is made with vegetable shortening instead of meringue.

(**FERNANDO** *walks in with a cake box.*)

FERNANDO. I thinks it's going to snow.

ROSITA. That would be a miracle, yes?

BARBARA. No, a very late winter. They say after this storm passes, it will be spring.

FERNANDO. Spring, imagine spring.

BARBARA. Yes.

ROSITA. A miracle.

BARBARA. No, air currents.

FERNANDO. You're losing all your sense of romance.

BARBARA. I listen to the weather man, that's all.

FERNANDO. Here is your cake, and I got fifteen candles.

ROSITA. I'm going to see how Rolando is doing in the kitchen. We are making a "Down with Fidel" feast and celebrating your sweet fifteen. This is going to be the biggest social event we've had in the U.S.A.

FERNANDO. What's the smell?

ROSITA. Roast pork. We bought a whole pig.

BARBARA. With the head and everything.

ROSITA. Yes!

FERNANDO. Smells like heaven.

ROSITA. Now that you bought Olga the Ford, we can shop in the Mexican part of town. They eat whole pigs, too. They call it "carnitas." They eat it on a soft corn tortilla with cilantro. Isn't that fascinating?

BARBARA. Exotic.

ROSITA. We are also having black beans.

BARBARA. Rosita, you are a miracle.

ROSITA. Found them in the Mexican part of town also.

FERNANDO. Mexicanos, compadres.

(**FERNANDO** and **ROSITA** laugh.)

BARBARA. I guess we have a lot of things in common with them.

ROSITA. We were conquered by the same people, that's all.

(**FERNANDO** takes the cake out of the box.)

FERNANDO. Beautiful, huh?

BARBARA. Kind of looks like Styrofoam.

ROSITA. A girl expects a white cake at her coming out party.

FERNANDO. At least it's chocolate.

BARBARA. In the US. Stick with chocolate. Can't ruin chocolate.

ROSITA. True.

FERNANDO. I saw a frozen puddle right outside on the front lawn. That's how cold it is today. In Cuba, water just made humidity, bred mosquitos. Here it turns into diamonds.

ROSITA. Ice.

BARBARA. It's like glass and when you step on it, it sounds like you are breaking someone's neck.

FERNANDO. Where's your Mother?

ROSITA. Getting ready for the ball. You'll explain it to her, Barbara.

BARBARA. What?

ROSITA. That you don't want to wear this dress.

BARBARA. Okay.

ROSITA. Yes?

BARBARA. I'll wear it as long as this is a rehearsal. Not the real thing.

ROSITA. Deal?

BARBARA. Deal.

ROSITA. When you get to Cuba, your grandfather is going to throw you a six thousand dollar coming out party.

BARBARA. Is that what he said in his letter?

ROSITA. Yes.

BARBARA. Wow! And all of my friends will be there. I want to come out in my own society. Not this one. And I want a cake from "La Gran Via," with rum in it. I'll get dressed.

(**BARBARA** *leaves.*)

FERNANDO. Did he really say that?

ROSITA. No.

FERNANDO. I thought so.

ROSITA. They're in the middle of being attacked. They have other things on their minds.

FERNANDO. Who could blame them?

ROSITA. Are we going to win, Fernando?

(**OLGA** *enters, she is wearing a beautiful low cut evening dress. Something she bought from Cuba. And some of her jewels.*)

OLGA. Of course we are going to win. The US is backing us, and the USA never loses.

FERNANDO. You look incredible.

OLGA. If the Presbyterians could see me now.

ROSITA. They'd faint.

FERNANDO. The jewels go back to the bacnk tomorrow, right?

OLGA. Yes.

FERNANDO. Good.

OLGA. Sister, why don't you wear some of the jewelry too?

ROSITA. Not with this outfit. The pork...

OLGA. I'll help you.

ROSITA. I want to do this myself. Rolando!

> *(***ROSITA*** exits.)*

OLGA. Here's your wife, do you recognize me?

FERNANDO. No matter what you're wearing, I recognize you.

> *(They kiss.* **ROLANDO** *enters.)*

ROLANDO. She needs you in the kitchen. She thinks we are overcooking the pork.

FERNANDO. There's no way to overcook pork.

OLGA. Yes there is.

ROLANDO. Just tell me what to tell her. You shouldn't cook, you are all dressed up.

OLGA. I was taught how to cook without getting my gown dirty. Help Fernando light the candles.

> *(***OLGA*** exits. They start to light the candles.)*

ROLANDO. Any more news?

FERNANDO. No.

ROLANDO. The US will be in there soon.

FERNANDO. As soon as that happens it's all over for Fidel.

ROLANDO. Amen!

FERNANDO. Yeah!

ROLANDO. What if the invasion lasts longer than a couple of days?

FERNANDO. It won't.

ROLANDO. But if it does? Do we go and fight and give up our jobs?

FERNANDO. As soon as the air strikes come, it is all over. Twenty-four hours.

ROLANDO. Are you going to go back right away?

FERNANDO. I'm going to send Olga on the first plane. Then I'm going to take my time and think.

ROLANDO. Think what?

FERNANDO. If I could ever belong there again.

ROLANDO. I'll send my wife straight from Miami. Save the ticket to Dallas.

FERNANDO. I like it here. They love my Latin looks, Rolando.

ROLANDO. The secretaries?

FERNANDO. And the clients. Here, I have magic in my eyes. There, I'm my father's son.

ROLANDO. I know what you mean. Here I'm not the poor relative.

(**OLGA** *enters with incense. She circles the men.*)

OLGA. For good luck.

ROLANDO. Santeria.

FERNANDO. You do that voodoo that you do so well.

OLGA. My mother sent it to me in a letter. So we could ask the Saints for freedom.

ROLANDO. It smells.

(**FERNANDO** *goes to the record player. He puts on Nat King Cole's Cuban album. He goes over to* **OLGA.**)

OLGA. Even Nat King Cole knows our music is the best.

FERNANDO. It's the only Cuban record I could find.

ROLANDO. Beny More is better.

(*She gives* **ROLANDO** *the incense. He places it on top of the television set and does the sign of the cross.* **FER-NANDO** *and* **OLGA** *dance.* **ROLANDO** *finishes lighting the candles.* **BARBARA** *walks in wearing her white dress.*

She looks beautiful.)

ROLANDO. Jesus, cousins! Your daughter has turned into a princess.

OLGA. Yes she has.

FERNANDO. In my eyes she's always been a beauty. I'm glad I didn't have any more children. I knew that no other child your mother and I ever manufactured could ever be as beautiful as you.

OLGA. Yes. And, my little beauty, here is something from the treasures of the ocean to place in your ears.

*(**OLGA** shows her the larger pearl earrings.)*

ROLANDO. You are going to spoil her.

BARBARA. I can wear them?

FERNANDO. Of course.

BARBARA. Thank you, Papi.

*(**BARBARA** starts to put on her earrings. **OLGA** helps her.)*

OLGA. I wish mother could see you.

BARBARA. She will Mama.

OLGA. Yes.

FERNANDO. And real soon.

BARBARA. It will be wonderful.

OLGA. They fit your personality perfectly.

BARBARA. It feels so good to have them on!

OLGA. Nothing like the genuine article.

ROLANDO. Dance with me, cousin?

OLGA. I'll lead.

*(They all dance. **ROSITA** enters.)*

ROSITA. Alright. It's time for a good luck toast, then your official coming out waltz, then a "Beat the Son of a Bitch" roast pork event...God, will I pull this off?

OLGA. It's almost time for the news.

*(**OLGA** turns on the television.)*

OLGA. Translate this for me, Barbara.

BARBARA. You understand, Mama.

ROSITA. Open the bottle of champagne, Rolando.

OLGA. Not from the television.

BARBARA. You should try to figure out what they are saying.

ROSITA. Tonight the celebration is for Cuba. To remember all the things we miss.

ROLANDO. Here.

(He begins to hand people glasses.)

FERNANDO. Not Barbara.

ROSITA. It's her coming out party.

ROLANDO. Let her drink it, Fernando.

FERNANDO. She's only fifteen.

ROLANDO. It's the only way to teach a girl not to be a cheap date.

FERNANDO. Hey! That's my daughter you're talking about.

ROLANDO. It was a joke.

FERNANDO. It's against the law here.

OLGA. Then drink it.

FERNANDO. Let's break their drinking laws. Great, fine!

BARBARA. I'm gonna like it.

(They raise their glasses; the news has started on the television.)

ALL. Down with Fidel! And happy birthday!

TELEVISION. "And now on the international front in Cuba..."

OLGA. Quick, he said Cuba, listen.

TELEVISION. "The invasion to overthrow Castro which began three days ago has failed. Fidel Castro has succeeded in stopping an overthrow to his government. The Castro regime claims that the only survivors of the invasion surrendered Thursday after being trapped in the south coast swamps. Executions of conspirators have begun. Havana was quiet again on Thursday night. Meanwhile in New York, leaders of the Cuban Revolutionary Council conceded today their cause had suffered "a grave reverse" but said the fight to free Cuba will go on until the end."

ROSITA. Turn it off!

TELEVISION. "The atmosphere in Havana, and apparently also in provincial cities, is one of tension underlying calm..."

FERNANDO. Yes.

(He turns off the television. Everyone is quiet.)

OLGA. "The fight to free Cuba will go on until the end." I understood that.

BARBARA. It can't be over.

*(**BARBARA** starts to cry.)*

FERNANDO. Please Barbara, don't cry.

OLGA. Why didn't people go out into the streets. What happened to the air support. Where are the Marines?

ROSITA. It's over.

OLGA. No, the fight to free Cuba will go on until the end!

BARBARA. I'm never going to "come out."

ROSITA. It's so sad, and I wanted the party to be wonderful.

OLGA. Fernando! We have to do something.

FERNANDO. Olga, the invasion failed. Fidel is still in power. Those are the facts. But we must survive past tonight. We must.

OLGA. No, the fight to free Cuba will go on until the end. That's all I know.

ROLANDO. Poor sons of bitches. No air support. Set up. They were set up.

FERNANDO. Aren't you glad I didn't let you go?

ROLANDO. Thank you.

OLGA. You didn't let him go?

FERNANDO. That's right. Not worth losing your life for –

OLGA. Your country?

FERNANDO. That's right.

OLGA. Yes it is. You promised me!

FERNANDO. To fight.

OLGA. Yes.

FERNANDO. Not to die. Not to die. I never promised to die for that little island.

OLGA. Rolando it's not over, go back. Go there now and fight. Be a man!

ROLANDO. It's over for now, cousin. It's over for now.

(**FERNANDO** *takes his champagne glass and raises it.*)

OLGA. Our dream's been killed.

ROLANDO. Dreams mean nothing, just movies while we sleep.

FERNANDO. A toast.

OLGA. To what?

FERNANDO. Survival.

OLGA. I don't want to survive here.

FERNANDO. You're going to have to.

OLGA. I can't toast to a future here, I won't!

ROSITA. Let's try a simple toast. Let there still be hope.

ROLANDO. Yes, to hope.

BARBARA. Mama, can I toast to that?

ROSITA. We are all going to toast to that.

OLGA. I am going back. I am going back to Cuba!

FERNANDO. We have to stay here. We are going to make the best with what we have in this place. Understand?

OLGA. You're relieved that you don't have to go back?

FERNANDO. In a way.

OLGA. You have no pride.

FERNANDO. What's a country, Olga! What's a country?

OLGA. What's a country? The place you're meant to wake up in. The place where your nature compliments the surroundings. Your definition on earth. The landscape your eyes were trained to see. The air your lungs like to breathe.

FERNANDO. That's not true.

OLGA. You are a coward. My father told me you were a coward!

FERNANDO. I have the right to make a new life.

OLGA. I don't want a new life. I had a life. I'm going.

FERNANDO. I'll lock you up in an insane asylum before I let you go back!

OLGA. You can't stop me!

FERNANDO. Yes I can. You are my wife.

BARBARA. Not your servant!

FERNANDO. What?

BARBARA. Women have a right to not be subservient to men.

FERNANDO. Who told you that?

BARBARA. The Presbyterian next door. She has her own checking account. And her husband does the dishes every other day.

FERNANDO. Well, he's a fool.

ROLANDO. An American.

ROSITA. Look, the news has got to get better. I think we are overreacting. I think we should have the buffet. Help me set it up, Olga.

OLGA. No.

ROSITA. Please.

OLGA. Sister, help me!

ROSITA. Come into the kitchen.

OLGA. No.

BARBARA. I'll help you.

ROLANDO. So will I.

(They exit.)

FERNANDO. You're scaring everybody.

OLGA. I'm...

FERNANDO. Out of control?

OLGA. No.

FERNANDO. Let me get you a Vallum.

OLGA. No. I'm angry. I want to be angry.

FERNANDO. I want my wife the way she used to be.

OLGA. You do? She lives in Cuba!

(ROSITA *enters with the roasted pig on a platter. The rest follow with more food.*)

ROSITA. Ta-dum. The feast.

OLGA. The "we lost the war" feast?

ROSITA. A battle, not the war. We have to believe that. And it never got near La Habana. So it means Mama and Papa and our ten thousand cousins are safe.

ROLANDO. Amen!

FERNANDO. I'm going to eat.

OLGA. You're hungry?

FERNANDO. I'm really hungry.

OLGA. You bastard. I've lived in Texas for months. Pretending to be a Presbyterian. Knowing that to them I look like a freak, not acceptable, not trustworthy. Foreign. A Martian. But I did it because you promised me. You promised me you would fight.

FERNANDO. You are out of control. I don't speak with women when they are out of control.

OLGA. I don't fit here. I was brought up for something different.

ROSITA. So was I.

(ROSITA *goes to the window.*)

ROLANDO. She was, Fernando. She had all the virtues. She did. The pride of my entire family. She had gotten us to the top. She was society.

FERNANDO. We were all brought up for something different!

OLGA. No, you trained yourself to adapt, to be ready to adapt. I was trained to be taken care of, now take care of me!

(*It starts to snow.*)

ROSITA. It's snowing. Snow.

BARBARA. It's a miracle.

ROSITA. Look, pieces of frozen water falling from the sky.

ROLANDO. How beautiful it looks.

FERNANDO. My god snow. Snow.

ROSITA. They look like ballerinas.

ROLANDO. I'm going out.

FERNANDO. Olga, Olga please.

OLGA. Go out and enjoy it.

FERNANDO. Barbara?

BARBARA. No thank you. I'm going to listen to the news.

FERNANDO. After the news.

BARBARA. I'll do whatever makes you happy.

FERNANDO. I'll give you five minutes, if you're not out I'll come back in and get you.

(**FERNANDO** *exits.*)

BARBARA. Okay.

ROSITA. The pork is going to have to be re-heated.

BARBARA. Later.

(**BARBARA** *opens a window and looks at the snow.* **ROSITA** *stands by her.*)

ROSITA. I wonder if it's cold?

(**ROSITA** *sticks her hand out the window.*)

ROSITA. It's like catching butterflies.

OLGA. Is it?

ROSITA. Try it?

OLGA. Alright.

ROSITA. Close your eyes when you do it.

OLGA. Fine. It feels like the fish nibbling when we fed them.

ROSITA. I forgot all about our aquariums.

OLGA. They were tropical fish.

ROSITA. Yes.

OLGA. Tropical life, pampered. Needs just the right temperature in the water, warm and gentle.

BARBARA. Look at them playing in the snow. They forgot they're tropical.

OLGA. Rosita, am I just a spoilt bitch?

ROSITA. If you are... Fidel was right about us.

OLGA. So, am I?

BARBARA. No! You're not, Mama.

(**ROLANDO** *walks in. He is covered in snow.*)

BARBARA. You look like a snow man.

ROLANDO. I feel like one.

ROSITA. How cold is it?

ROLANDO. Not as cold as you would think, for ice.

ROSITA. Really?

ROLANDO. Barbara, your father says your five minutes are up.

BARBARA. Mama?

OLGA. Enjoy yourself.

BARBARA. I'm ready. I'm ready, yes!

ROSITA. Get a coat.

(**BARBARA** *goes to get a coat.*)

ROLANDO. Coming with us?

OLGA. No.

ROLANDO. Rosita?

ROSITA. Well?

OLGA. Yes, she is.

ROSITA. I'll get my coat.

(**ROSITA** *exits.* **OLGA** *starts to fill a plate with food.*)

ROLANDO. Cousin, later if you want me to set him straight, I will. We'll go back and fight for Cuba. I'll be there with a gun and hand grenades. You can count on me.

OLGA. Yes. Right. I'm sure.

(**BARBARA** *and* **ROSITA** *are there.*)

BARBARA. I'm going to make a snow angel. I read about it in a book.

OLGA. Don't fall in the snow.

(They all exit.)

Eat, Olga, eat. Eat, it'll bring you back there.

(She eats. We hear them playing outside. FERNANDO *enters. He goes up to her.)*

FERNANDO. Forgive me.

*(*OLGA *takes off her wedding rings.)*

OLGA. Sell my wedding rings.

FERNANDO. Are you sure?

OLGA. Yes. Pay back the poor Presbyterians and send a check to the Catholic relief. I'm sure they need money to help other families who will be arriving in Miami after tonight. And I'm going to go and ask for my job back.

FERNANDO. That's the spirit. In a couple of years. I'll buy you back better ones. You'll have a bigger diamond on your hand.

OLGA. It doesn't matter.

FERNANDO. I knew you'd pull through.

OLGA. You're happy?

FERNANDO. Happy for us, sad for our country. If I work really hard this year, we will be able to move out of this shit hole. Get a house with a pool.

OLGA. We are no longer the children.

FERNANDO. No, we are not.

OLGA. I didn't want to grow up.

FERNANDO. We have to.

OLGA. I'm hungry.

FERNANDO. There's always later for food. Come out and play. Barbara would like that.

OLGA. Go. I'll be out there soon.

FERNANDO. Thank you.

(They kiss.)

FERNANDO. What was that song? It was about snow.

*(He exits. **OLGA** eats.)*

OLGA. I'm beginning to forget.... Yes...yes...

*(**OLGA** removes her brooch and she pins herself. **BAR-BARA** has walked in.)*

BARBARA. Where are you?

OLGA. Christmas Eve ... Mama...the smell of Mama's hands when she had put garlic, bitter oranges and oregano on the pork. Wait for me, Mama. Please wait for me.

BARBARA. Give me the pin. I need to prick myself.

OLGA. No, show me how to play in the snow.

BARBARA. Really?

OLGA. Yes.

*(**BARBARA** goes to get the coat. **OLGA** eats.)*

BARBARA. Snow is beautiful, almost like the sand of Varadero, but cold.

OLGA. Is it?

*(**OLGA** puts on her coat.)*

BARBARA. Yes. This is so exciting.

OLGA. Let's go.

BARBARA. Button your coat.

OLGA. Let's walk in the snow.

*(**OLGA** starts to button her coat. They walk out into the snow.)*

End of play

Also by
Eduardo Machado...

Broken Eggs

The Cook

Eye of the Hurricane

Havana is Waiting

Kissing Fidel

Modern Ladies of Guanabacoa

Once Removed

OTHER TITLES AVAILABLE FROM SAMUEL FRENCH

DEAD CITY
Sheila Callaghan

Full Length / Comic Drama / 3m, 4f / Unit Set
It's June 16, 2004. Samantha Blossom, a chipper woman in her 40s, wakes up one June morning in her Upper East Side apartment to find her life being narrated over the airwaves of public radio. She discovers in the mail an envelope addressed to her husband from his lover, which spins her raw and untethered into an odyssey through the city… a day full of chance encounters, coincidences, a quick love affair, and a fixation on the mysterious Jewel Jupiter. Jewel, the young but damaged poet genius, eventually takes a shine to Samantha and brings her on a midnight tour of the meat-packing district which changes Samantha's life forever—or doesn't. This 90 minute comic drama is a modernized, gender-reversed, relocated, hyper-theatrical riff on the novel Ulysses, occurring exactly 100 years to the day after Joyce's jaunt through Dublin.

"Wonderful… Sheila Callaghan's pleasingly witty and theatrical new drama that is a love letter to New York masquerading as hate mail… [Callaghan] writes with a world-weary tone and has a poet's gift for economical description.
The entire dead city comes alive…"
- *New York Times*

"*Dead City,* Sheila Callaghan's riff on James Joyce's Ulysses is stylish, lyrical, fascinating, occasionally irritating, and eminently worthwhile… the kind of work that is thoroughly invigorating."
- *Backstage*

OTHER TITLES AVAILABLE FROM SAMUEL FRENCH

JACK GOES BOATING
Bob Glaudini

Full Length / Comedy / 2m, 2f / Interior

Four flawed but likeable lower-middle-class New Yorkers interact in a touching and warmhearted play about learning how to stay afloat in the deep water of day-to-day living. Laced with cooking classes, swimming lessons and a smorgasbord of illegal drugs, *Jack Goes Boating* is a story of date panic, marital meltdown, betrayal, and the prevailing grace of the human spirit.

"An immensely likable play [that] exudes a wry compassion."
- The New York Times

"Endearing romantic comedy about a married couple and the social-misfit friends they fix up. Witty and knowing and all heart."
- Variety

"Glides effortlessly from the shallow end of the emotional pool to the deep end."
- Theatremania.com